P9-DMI-527

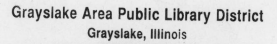

if Beaver had a fever

by Helen Ketteman

illustrated by

Kevin O'Malley

Marshall Cavendish Children

Text copyright © 2011 by Helen Ketteman
Illustrations copyright © 2011 by Kevin O'Malley

Marshall Cavendish Corporation, 99 White Plains Road, Tarrytown, NY 10591
www.marshallcavendish.us/kids

Library of Congress Cataloging-in-Publication Data
Ketteman, Helen.
If Beaver had a fever / by Helen Ketteman ; illustrated by Kevin O'Malley.—1st ed.
p. cm.
Summary: Little Bear learns that if he becomes sick, Mama Bear will nurse him, and a variety of zoo animals, back to health.
ISBN 978-0-7614-5951-4 (hardcover) — ISBN 978-0-7614-5998-9 (ebook)
[1. Stories in rhyme. 2. Sick—Fiction. 3. Mother and child—Fiction. 4. Bears—Fiction. 5. Zoo animals—Fiction.] I. O'Malley, Kevin,
1961– ill. II. Title.
PZ8.3.K46If 2011
[E]—dc22
2010044928

The illustrations are rendered in art markers, colored pencils, and crayons.
Book design by Anahid Hamparian
Editor: Marilyn Brigham

Printed in China (E)
First edition
10 9 8 7 6 5 4 3 2 1

For Anne Ketteman, with lots of love
—H.K.

For Anahid Hamparian,
a great art director and fabulous humorist
—K.O.

"Mama Bear, Mama Bear!"

"Yes, Little Bear?"

"If you were a doctor
in charge of the zoo,
what would you do
if Gnu had the flu?"

"If Gnu came to my office,
with aches and a chill,
I'd bake him a cake
chockfull of pills."

"If Chimp came to see me,
and his foot had a pain,
I'd tell him to walk
with a big candy cane."

"If Deer came complaining
that she couldn't hear,
I'd stick a BIG megaphone
into each ear."

"If Meerkat came by
weighing too many pounds,
I'd call over Cheetah
to chase him around."

"If Fox came to see me
all splotchy and red,
I'd pull a striped sweatshirt
right over her head."

"If Beaver came over
and his fever went up,
I'd give him ice cream
in a GIGANTIC cup."

"What if
Weasel had
the measles?"

"If Weasel showed up
with spots and an itch,
I'd tell him to roll
around in the ditch."

"But Mama Bear, Mama Bear,
how would you be
if you were a doctor,
and the sick one were me?"

"I'd puppet a story.
I'd tootle a tune.
I'd huff and I'd puff you
a big red balloon."

"We'd play board games,
then cuddle awhile.
I'd tickle your piggies
to get you to smile."

"I'd fix all your favorites—
cookies and soup—
and when you got better,
I'd let out a WHOOOOP!"

"So if my Little Bear's sick,
there's nothing to fear."

"Whatever goes wrong,
your Mama Bear's here."